SO MANY BUNNIES

a bedtime abc

and counting

book

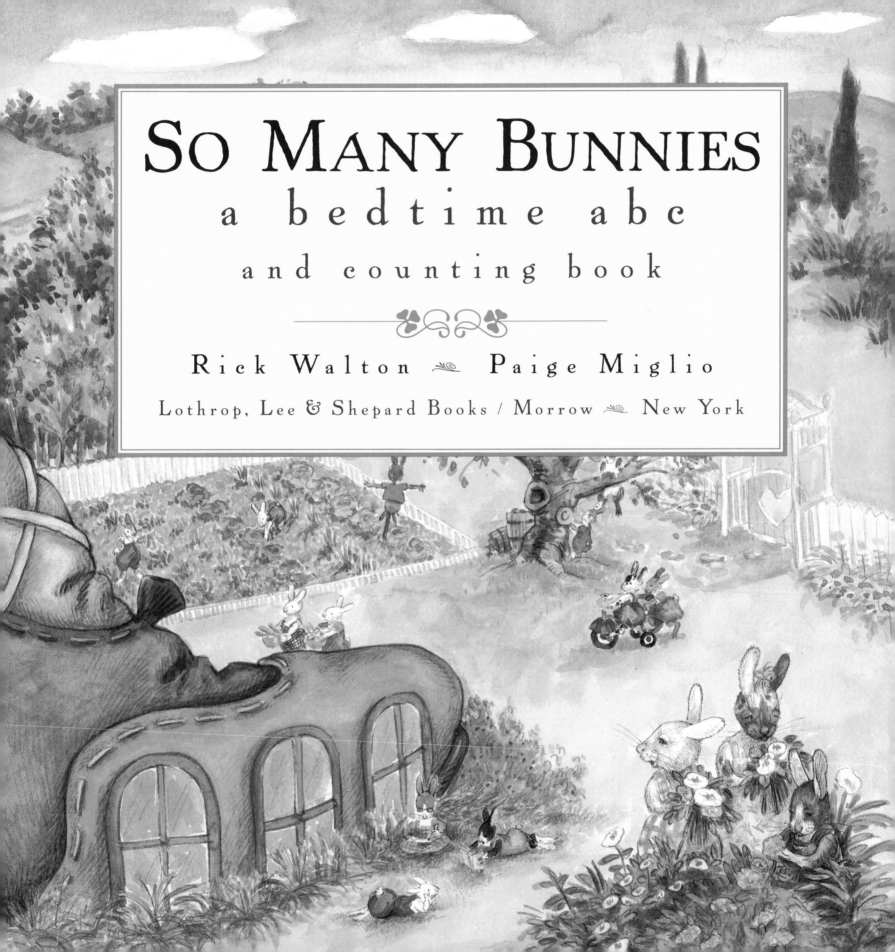

SO MANY BUNNIES

a bedtime abc

and counting book

Rick Walton ✥ Paige Miglio

Lothrop, Lee & Shepard Books / Morrow ✥ New York

Old Mother Rabbit lived in a shoe.
She had twenty-six children and knew what to do.
She fed them some carrots, some broth, and some bread,
Then kissed them all gently and put them to bed.

1 was named Abel.
He slept on the table.

2 was named **B**lair.
She slept in a chair.

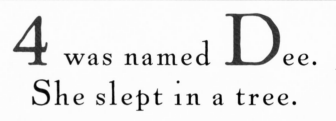

4 was named Dee.
She slept in a tree.

3 was named Carol.
She slept in a barrel.

5 was named Ellis.
He slept on the trellis.

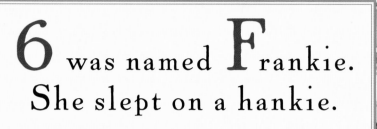

6 was named Frankie.
She slept on a hankie.

7 was named Gretel.
She slept in the kettle.

8 was named Hank.
He slept with his bank.

9 was named **I**ke.
He slept on his trike.

10 was named **J**ane.
She slept in the lane.

11 was named **K**ate.
She slept on the gate.

12 was named **L**ink.
He slept in the sink.

13 was named **M**andy.
She slept in the candy.

14 was named **N**oel.
He slept in a bowl.

15 was named **O**llie.
He slept by the holly.

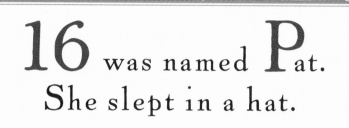

16 was named Pat.
She slept in a hat.

17 was named Quinn.
He slept in a bin.

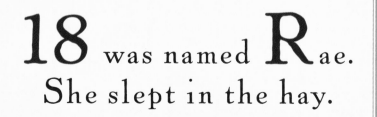

18 was named **R**ae.
She slept in the hay.

19 was named **S**am.
He slept with his lamb.

20 was named **T**oni. She slept with her pony.

21 was named **U**te.
He slept by the fruit.

22 was named **V**ern.
He slept by a fern.

23 was named **W**illow.
She slept on a pillow.

24 was named Xen.
He slept with his pen.

25 was named **Y**ale.
He slept by the scale.

LETTER

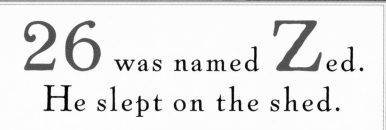

26 was named Zed. He slept on the shed.

Old Mother Rabbit lived in a shoe.
She had twenty-six children and plenty to do.
She tucked them all in, from Abel to Zed,
Then curled herself up in a soft feather bed.

To Evan and Betty Jo Ivie, who had many children and knew what to do.
—RW

To my baby bunny, Marcus, and his brothers Nathan and Noel and Jeremy.
And to the "Mother Bunny," Judy Sue.
—PM

Pen-and-ink over watercolors was used for the full-color illustrations. The text type is 24-point Powell Old Style.

Text copyright © 1998 by Rick Walton
Illustrations copyright © 1998 by Paige Miglio

Published by Lothrop, Lee & Shepard Books
an imprint of Morrow Junior Books
a division of William Morrow and Company, Inc.
1350 Avenue of the Americas, New York, NY 10019
www.williammorrow.com

Printed in the United States of America.

1 2 3 4 5 6 7 8 9 10

Library of Congress Cataloging-in-Publication Data
Walton, Rick.
So many bunnies: a bedtime abc and counting book / by Rick Walton; illustrated by Paige Miglio.
p. cm.
Summary: Old Mother Rabbit's twenty-six children, each named for a letter of the alphabet, are lovingly put to bed.
ISBN 0-688-13656-7 (trade)—ISBN 0-688-13657-5 (library)
[1. Bedtime—Fiction. 2. Rabbits—Fiction. 3. Alphabet. 4. Counting. 5. Stories in rhyme.]
I. Miglio, Paige, ill. II. Title. PZ8.3.W199So 1998 [E]—dc21 97-6471 CIP AC